WOLFIE
THE BUNNY

D0551347

ANDERSEN PRESS

Written by **Ame Dyckman**   Illustrated by **Zachariah OHora**

The Bunny family came home to find
a bundle outside their door.

They peeked. They gasped. It was a baby wolf!
"He's adorable!" said Mama. "He's ours!" said Papa.

"HE'S GOING TO EAT US ALL UP!"

said Dot.

But Mama and Papa were too smitten to listen.

Wolfie slept through the night.

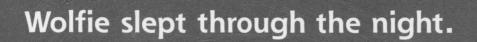

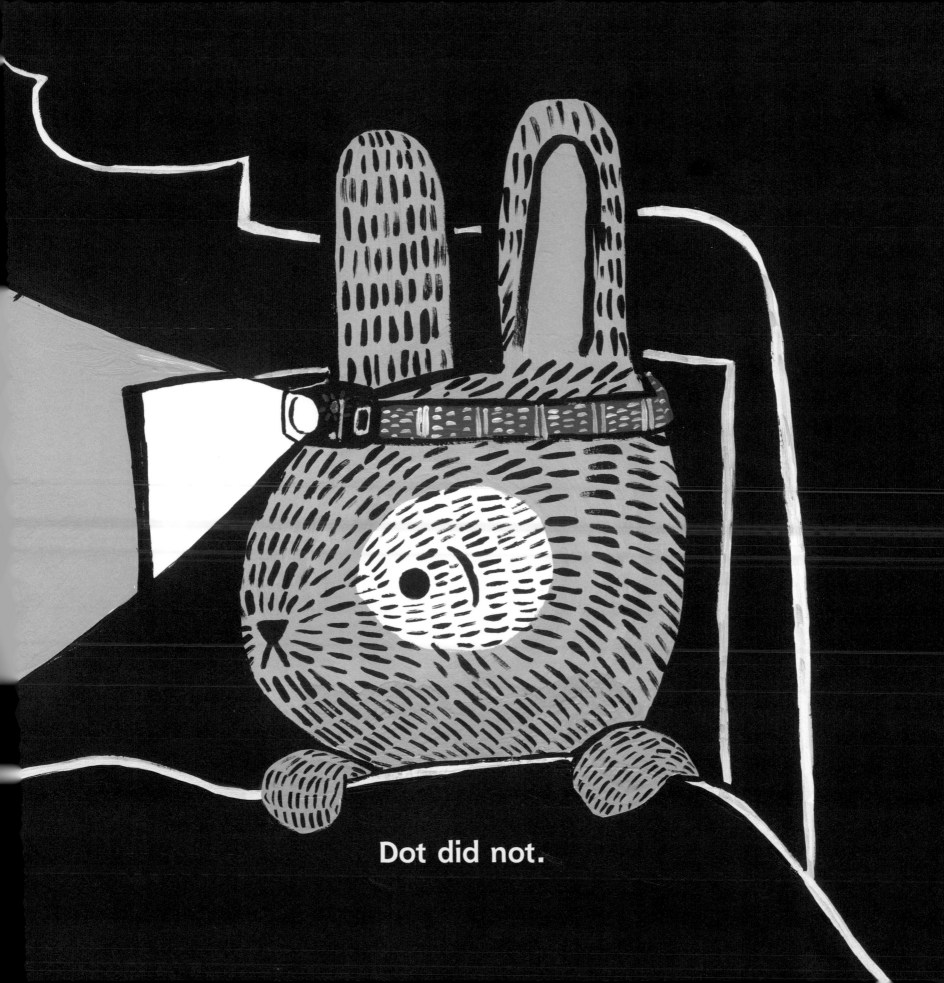

Dot did not.

Mama served carrots for breakfast.
"He likes them!" said Mama.

"He's a good eater!" said Papa.

"Speaking of eating," said Dot,

"HE'S GOING TO EAT US ALL UP!"

But Mama and Papa were too busy
taking pictures to listen.

Dot's friends came by to see the baby.

"He's sleeping," whispered Mama.
"He's a good sleeper," whispered Papa.

"HE'S GOING TO EAT US ALL UP!"

they screamed.

"Yep," said Dot.
"Let's play at your house."

For the first time, Wolfie cried.

But Dot was too far away to hear him.

When Dot returned,
Wolfie was waiting.

Everywhere Dot went,
Wolfie went, too.

"He's dribbling on me!"
said Dot.

"He's a good dribbler!"
said Papa.

The days passed, and Wolfie grew.
So did his appetite.

When Mama opened the cupboard, she got a surprise.
"The carrots!" said Mama. "They're gone!"
"Oh no!" said Papa.

"HE ATE THEM ALL UP!"
said Dot.

Dot fetched the carrot bag.
But she did not get far.

Wolfie and Dot went to the Carrot Patch.

Dot was picking one last carrot when Wolfie's mouth opened wide.

"I *knew* it!" cried Dot.

"On guard!"

But Wolfie wasn't looking at Dot.

"DINNER!"

roared the bear.

It was Dot's chance to run away.

Instead, she ran forward.

"Let him go!" Dot demanded.

"Or... I'LL EAT YOU ALL UP!"

The bear blinked. "You're a bunny," he said.

"I'M A HUNGRY BUNNY," said Dot.

"But I'm bigger than you,"
said the bear.

"I'LL START ON YOUR TOES,"
said Dot.

Dot relaxed as the bear ran away.
"We're safe!" she said.

Then Wolfie pounced.

"Come on, little brother.
Let's go home and eat."

ARTIST'S NOTE

The illustrations in this book were painted in acrylic on 90-pound acid-free Stonehenge paper. The setting is an homage to my family's former neighborhood of Park Slope, Brooklyn, where we had a little "garden level" apartment — which is really New York real estate-speak for "You live in a basement." But what better place for a bunny family to live?

It was a sweet time for us as new parents, and I'm glad to capture some of that feeling in the art for this wonderful story.

—*Zachariah OHora*

AUTHOR'S NOTE

My daughter was an adorable toddler—except when she was tired. Then she transformed. "She's a Wolf Baby!" her father and I would say. (Quietly, so she wouldn't hear us.) And that gave me an idea...   —*Ame Dyckman*